Mrudul Tale

FAVORITE TALES FROM THE
PANCHATANTRA

Retold by: **MRUDUL TATA**
Illustrated by: **HOLLEY BENTON**

TATA PUBLISHING

First Impression 1994.

Printed in Hong Kong by South China Printing Company (1988) Ltd.

Library of Congress Catalog Card Number 93-94284

ISBN 0-9639913-0-2

INTRODUCTION

Long ago there lived an Indian King who had three sons. The princes were very dull and lazy. Many teachers were tried but the princes were unable to learn anything. Then one day a learned old man undertook the task of teaching them. He told them stories of birds and animals which the princes listened to very attentively and from the stories learned the art of living a life where friendship, trust and respect play a very important role. These ancient stories originally written in Sanskrit are the most popular and famous collection of short stories in the world today.

Dedicated to Ganesh, The God of Wisdom

CONTENTS

1.   The Lion and the Rabbit.

2.   The Stork and the Crab.

3.   The Blue Jackal.

THE LION AND THE RABBIT

Once upon a time there lived in a jungle a very fierce lion. All the animals were afraid of him because he was a very good hunter and had killed a lot of animals. They soon realized that before long there would not be any animals left in the jungle, so they decided to meet the lion.

"Your Majesty!" said one of the animals, "You are a King and you need subjects, but after a while you will have no subjects left. Since we want you to be our King forever we have a suggestion to make to you. We will send you one animal everyday for your dinner and this way, you will not have to hunt for food and you and the animals will live happily and in peace."

The lion thought it was a very good idea and then after thinking for a moment said, "I agree to listen to you but remember the day I do not get any food, I will kill as many animals as I possibly can."

The animals told him that they would keep their word and left.

The next day the lion had one animal for dinner without having to hunt for food. The day after was the turn of the rabbits. Now among the lot of rabbits was a very clever young rabbit. Since it was his turn to go and he did not want to be eaten he thought of a plan. He walked very slowly to the lion's den. The lion having waited for his food all day was absolutely furious by the time he saw the rabbit.

"Where have you been?" he asked the rabbit.

"As it is you are too small for my dinner and you are late," he roared.

The rabbit was very scared but nevertheless bowing low very politely said, "Oh, Great One, the animals had in fact sent six rabbits but another lion ate five of the rabbits on our way here."

"What!" roared the lion, "Another lion in this jungle! Where did you see him?"

"Oh!" said the rabbit very cunningly, "He is a very fierce lion and he wanted to eat me too, but I told him that if he did not let me go he will have to deal with you, Our King! Hearing this he got very angry and asked me to fetch you so that he could see you, because he thinks you are an imposter. He has let me go so that I could take you to him. I am sorry I am late but I ran as fast as my little legs could carry me."

On hearing this the lion got absolutely angry. So furious was he, that the entire jungle shook with his roar.

"Take me to the place where this imposter lives," he said to the rabbit, "and I will kill him!"

The rabbit was very smart, he led the lion to a big well in the jungle.

"Where is he?" asked the lion looking around.

"Oh, he is in there!" said the rabbit pointing towards the well.

The lion went to the well and looked in. He saw his own reflection in the water. Upon seeing it he got very angry and roared very loudly. When he roared the echo of the roar from inside was louder than his own roar. Without thinking he jumped into the well to attack his enemy and crashed his head against the rocks and fell in the water and died.

The rabbit then returned to the jungle and told the animals that they could live in peace since he had got rid of the lion once and for all.

THE STORK AND THE CRAB

A stork lived by the side of a lake for a very long time. In the lake lived all kinds of beautiful fish which the stork enjoyed eating everyday. As the years went by the stork got old and weary and found it very difficult to catch the fish. Fearing he would die of starvation he thought of a plan.

For days he stood by the side of the lake looking very sad and did not try to catch any fish. The fish, frogs and crabs that swam by noticed how sad the stork looked and wondered what happened to him.

One day, one of the crabs that lived with the fish in the lake went up to the stork and said, "My friend, why have you not been fishing for food ? Why are you so sad?"

The stork replied with a heavy sigh, "I have spent all my life by the side of this lake and was able to catch fish for dinner, but now things are going to change. All the fish in this lake are going to die."

"Why?" asked the crab very scared for his life.

"Because," said the stork, "I heard people say that they are going to do away with this lake and fill it with mud and dirt and grow crops here."

When the crabs and fish heard the stork's lies they were very frightened for their life. Concerned about their future and safety and not realizing how sly he was, they said to the stork, "Oh, Noble One, knowing how wise you are, could you think of a way to help save us all?"

The stork smiled and thought to himself, "These fish would make a very good dinner for me and they will all be at my mercy." Then pretending to be very serious he said, "I am only a bird, but I will help save you in any possible way I can.   A little distance away from this lake is another lake where I can take you, and you will all be safe."

"Take me first, take me first!" cried the fish in the lake all at once.

"Have patience," said the stork, "I am old and weary and therefore do things very slowly. I can take only one fish at a time but I shall make as many trips as possible."

And so he started carrying the fish one by one in his bill out of the lake to the top of a distant rock.

There he ate the fish, rested for a while and then returned to the lake.

Every day he followed this routine until there were very few fish left in the lake. Still left in the lake was the crab, who was very scared. He asked the stork to take him to the lake as well with the rest of the fish.

The stork by then was tired of eating fish. He thought he might try the crab for a change, so he said to the crab, "Come on my friend, I am here to help you, let me carry you to the other lake."

So saying he picked the crab up by its leg in his bill and flew up in the air.

After they flew for a while the crab noticed that there was no water in sight and the stork was ready to land on a large rock.

Wondering why there was no lake in sight he said to the stork, "My friend, where is the lake you were taking me to?"

The stork laughed wickedly and said, "Do you see that large rock down there, that is the place I am taking you to, and that is the place I took all the fish."

The crab looked down and to his horror saw the rock littered with heaps and heaps of fish bones. He immediately realized that he had been tricked by the cruel stork and knew that he would soon be dead if he did not do anything, so he thought hard.

Suddenly he turned and gripped his claws around the stork's neck and squeezed hard. The stork struggled and fell to the ground and died. The crab then returned to the lake.

When the rest of the fish saw the crab return they were surprised and asked him what had happened.

The crab then told them how the stork had cheated all the fish and eaten them and how he had put an end to him.

THE BLUE JACKAL

O nce upon a time there lived in a jungle, a jackal. One day while looking for food, tired and hungry he strayed into a city at nightfall.

"I've got to find food soon," he thought to himself. He knew it was dangerous for him to be in the city because he was attacked by men and dogs every time he was on the outskirts of the city.

Suddenly, he heard dogs barking. Afraid that they might attack him, he started running. Frightened for his life and not seeing where he was running, he ran straight into the backyard of a house and fell headlong into a barrel.

Now the house belonged to a dyer and he had all kinds of different colors stored in barrels. After the dogs had gone, when the jackal came out of the barrel he was surprised to see that he was blue all over. Not knowing what to do he went back to the jungle. When the other animals saw him they all ran away from him. They had never seen anyone or anything like him.

"Who is this?" they all whispered amongst themselves.

The jackal was very shrewd. He realized rather quickly that they were all afraid of him and were not sure how strong he was. So he said to them, "Don't be afraid, I am your King. God has sent me here to protect you."

The animals believed what he said and bowing very low to him said, "Your Majesty, we thank God for sending you to us, but please tell us what you would have each one of us do?"

"Well!" said the jackal, "You are all supposed to look after your King very well and provide him with all the food he needs."

"Certainly, Your Majesty!" said all the animals.

From then on when the lions, leopards or tigers made a kill they brought it to the jackal and he gave each one of them their share.

Time passed by and all the animals went to him for suggestions and the jackal would tell them what to do.

One day as he sat in the jungle holding court he heard a pack of jackals howling. Having kept away from the jackals for fear of being recognized, he was happy to hear them howling and his eyes filled with tears. Forgetting he was a King, he howled back.

On hearing him the animals immediately knew they had been cheated. "Why, he is a jackal!" they all cried in anger and rushed to tear him apart, but the jackal was already far ahead of them running for his dear life.